D1453185

FIVE THINGS ABOUT DRAGONFLIES

CHILDREN OF THE GLADES BOOK 1

L. B. Anne

JOA PRESS
SEMINOLE, FLORIDA

Five Things About Dragonflies

Contents

While inspired by real events, Five Things About Dragonflies is a work of fiction and does not claim to be historically accurate or portray factual events or relationships. References to historical events, real persons, and real places are used fictitiously and may not be factually accurate but rather fictionalized by the author.

When you see this symbol ❖ go to pages 104-108 and read more on the person or topic.

An Appreciation

BY DARALENE BELL

Emmy Award-Winning Evening News Anchor and Investigative Journalist

I am honored that my friend L. B. Anne asked me to write this foreword. You'll understand why, or at least I hope, once you get to the end of this foreword.

I first met L. B. Anne 13 years ago at the church I still call home, and much has changed for both of us since then. I'm now a wife and the mother of three sprouting boys. She was a mother when we met but is now a proud grandmother.

The man I was dating at the time of our meeting is now my husband, and admittedly told me back then that he was concerned about our meeting, noting that L. B. Anne was a God-fearing, pure and gentle soul whom he'd gotten to know through their work in the church band. He often questioned how our two polar opposite personalities might mesh, wondering if they might ever collide. What he didn't know, and perhaps I didn't at the time either, is that we had more in common than anyone knew.

You see, L. B. Anne is a purist, who sees the good in all people, but also seeks the truth. And that's where our personalities co-mingle. So, as it turns out, it's actually fitting that I introduce you to her latest work, to help you understand why she is an authority in this space of fictional work about actual events in African American and indigenous peoples' history.

It's a full-circle moment in that when I met L. B. Anne. She was likely seeking the truth about her own life, and so was I.

The truth about my heritage, my culture, and what it all meant as it relates to the person I'd become. For L. B. Anne, it was likely a journey of identifying the same. In our respective lives, we have now become truth-seekers of our history, acknowledging through our writings that our history seen and exposed in black and white matters not only for us, but for our children and our grandchildren.

L. B. Anne has written a tale that deeply explores a journey of our cultural past through the eyes of a child, in hopes that when our own children and grandchildren become adults, they will no longer have to wonder who they are because through works like this, they'll already know.

Dragonflies are born underwater and live in the dark. When one first emerges, it appears colorless and transparent. But when sunlight hits its body, it becomes beautiful, colorful, and magical.

Chapter One

Mia sighed as she watched droplets of rain hit the car window. "You said you were taking us somewhere fun today, Dad. Not having fun yet."

Her father turned the steering wheel and guided the car to the right of a highway fork. "Wait and see. You're going to love it."

Mia raised her voice and sang, "I don't know why my parents are dragging me out to the middle of nowhere in this weather."

"Singing the words doesn't make them any less rude," her mother said from the passenger front seat. "Is the world supposed to stop because of a little rain?"

"I don't know," Mia mumbled.

"You know the weather here in Florida. One moment it looks like a typhoon has hit us. The next, the sun is shining."

Mia placed her earbuds into her ears and rocked against the backseat. Her hand flew up, matching the beat of the music.

"Woo-ooo, woah-oh!" she sang.

Her best friend Paisley, who sat next to her, glanced over, shook her head, and went back to texting.

"Not today, Mia," her father said, squinting at her in the rearview mirror.

Mia squeezed her eyes shut and bobbed her head. "Woo-ooo, woah-oh!"

"Mia!" He reached behind the driver's seat, flapping his hand and trying to tap her knee.

She crossed her leg away from his reaching fingers and kept right on singing.

Her father reached further, and the car swerved, veering toward the shoulder of the road. Mia fell into Paisley, and Paisley slid against the door as a semi truck's horn blared at them.

"Michael!" her mother exclaimed, holding her chest.

"We're okay, we're okay," he said, assuring himself more than anybody else. He turned up the windshield wipers with a trembling hand. "I'm sorry, guys. Paisley, are you okay?"

Paisley playfully shoved Mia off of her. "Yes, sir. I'm good."

"Dad, keep your eyes on the road. 'Focus', like you always tell me to," said Mia. She went to grab her phone from her lap, but it wasn't there. "Oh, no! Where's my phone?"

She kicked at the bags on the floor and found it under the bag of empty nachos from a half hour earlier. She frowned at her phone. "Look what you did to Bethany." Bits of sand and lint covered the phone, but at least the screen wasn't cracked. "Thank you, thank you, thank you," she whispered.

Her mother watched her over her shoulder. "Bethany? Who's Beth—oh I get it. Paisley, please don't tell me you've named your phone too."

"Yep, she sure did," said Mia. "Mom, doesn't Daddy always turn the wheel in the direction he's looking? Like if he looks at a store to the left, the wheel turns left. Haven't you noticed? You've seen him do it, right?"

"No comment. Put your seatbelt on."

Mia's father glanced at her in the rearview mirror. "It wouldn't have happened if you weren't singing and didn't have those things in your ears turned up so loud that you couldn't hear me trying to get your attention."

"This is a long drive," Mia whined, scrolling through the songs on her phone. "I'm bored. Paisley has her earbuds in too. You didn't say anything about hers."

"*She* can still hear me, right Paisley?"

Paisley held her hand up, then went back to the game on her phone.

Her father smirked. "See?"

Mia adjusted the bud in her left ear. "You could at least let me sing, Dad."

"That wasn't singing. That was—I don't know what that was. Howling?" he asked his wife.

She covered her mouth to hide her grin and nodded.

He pointed out the windshield. "This is our exit. Look, you can see the building over the bridge."

Mia paused the song on her phone and leaned forward. The fronds of palm trees and thick oak branches surrounded the point of a metal roof up ahead. "That red one?"

Her father nodded as he guided the car over the bridge. "Yep. That's it. Through those woods."

Mia tapped Paisley's shoulder, pointing out the window. "We're almost there."

Paisley looked up from her game. "I heard. Did you see the Ferris wheel back there though? Maybe we can stop at the carnival too, if it stops raining."

"Is that the big surprise?" Mia asked her parents. "You're taking us to a carnival afterward? That's it, right, Dad?"

A smile crossed his lips. "Something better."

"What's better than a carnival?" Mia whispered to Paisley.

Paisley shrugged.

Mia relaxed on her seat and looked out the window at the sky, wondering what her parents had planned for her. The rain came down softer now, the drops no longer drumming on the car.

They pulled off the expressway at the next exit. A few minutes later, Mia watched acres and acres of orange groves on either side of the road glide by.

There were no other businesses or houses. If they hadn't just left the highway, Mia would've thought there was no civilization for miles around. The secluded road didn't even have a stripe or dotted line down the center to show what side vehicles should drive on.

After another ten minutes of driving, the patchwork of groves and fields ended. The car pulled through ten-foot-tall open gates and into an empty parking lot.

Her father parked the car next to the nearest walkway. "We're here."

Mia's stomach jolted and her heart ran faster. The road was probably deserted for a reason. They were out in the middle of nowhere and with no witnesses.

Paisley leaned toward Mia and whispered, "It looks like there's been a zombie attack and we're the last humans."

"I know, right? Did you bring your crochet hooks with you? We might need weapons."

Paisley giggled and straightened in her seat.

"How exciting. I've always wanted to visit this place," said Mia's mother, unbuckling her seatbelt. "And the rain stopped right on time."

Mia rolled down her window. "Yeah, but now it's so muggy. The mosquitos are going to be vicious. Is this place even open?"

"It sure is." Her father opened his door and hopped out.

Her mother and Paisley got out of the car too. Mia slowly stepped out of the backseat and closed the car door, taking in the dense underbrush, the tall oaks dripping with Spanish moss, and the palm trees.

"Why did I think this was going to look like the National Museum of African American History and Culture in Washington, DC that we went to? This place is out in the middle of nowhere."

"Because it's not the National Museum of African American History," her father said. "But it's still a museum and part of the culture of this family. And how did you know about the museum here?" He glanced at his wife.

"Useummay? Come on, I'm not five. That pig Latin stuff doesn't work anymore, and you guys whisper loudly."

Her father looked her over. "Pull your pants up or that cropped thing down—whatever you have to do so I don't see your midriff."

Mia tugged at her top. "I brought a jacket, but it's a hundred degrees out here."

"Put it on. There'll be air conditioning inside. And your hair—"

"It's just braids," said her mother.

"They're burgundy." He shook his head and walked toward the museum entrance.

Mia frowned and tugged at one of her locks. "It washes out."

Paisley grabbed a handful of her identical blue braids and fanned her neck with them. The girls always matched each other. Although today, Paisley wore a black oversized t-shirt with Batman's insignia.

Mia lowered her voice. "Mom, why is Dad acting so weird? He knew what I looked like before we left."

"It's this place. He wants to make a good impression," her mother whispered.

"Why?"

"It's really important to him."

"But, why?"

Her mother gave her a knowing look and patted her shoulder. "Family. You'll see."

Mia sulked as she grabbed her jacket from the car, then put it on and zipped it up. Her mother and Paisley had already joined her father walking toward the museum, so she jogged to catch up to them.

"Dad, so you're saying there's information about our ancestors here?"

"You know some of our history," her father said as they continued up the wet walk, and Mia jumped over the puddles. "But it's been distorted. There is a friendship—a unity—that took place right here on this land."

Mia stopped and took out her earbuds, then put them in her pocket. "Really? Here? Okay, I'm interested. Stop looking so proud of yourselves. Walk faster, old people."

"Watch it." Her mother gave her a sly look. "We're not old."

"This has to be the longest walkway ever," said Paisley. "Is that a little horse over there?"

"I think it's a cow. There were random cows in the fields all the way here." Mia walked ahead of everyone and pointed at a tree towering high above the building behind it. "Look at the size of that mango tree!"

"Yum," said Paisley.

They were used to the humidity in Southern Florida, but this day was especially muggy and made the trek to the museum entrance seem a mile away. Mia scratched at imaginary mosquito bites on her hands. Just being outside with the air so thick made her skin tingle like a hundred noseeums had bitten her.

Paisley hopped out of the way as geckos crossed back and forth over the path in front of the building. And just before Mia's father opened the door for them to enter, a dragonfly neared. Its wings were almost transparent, outlined in black with flecks of blue, bronze, and gold. Mia had always been fond of them. She watched in awe as it hovered over her head for a moment, then flew backward and zipped away.

"Okay, that was weird."

"What?" asked her mother.

"Nothing." She shook her head. "I think a dragonfly tried to eat me."

Paisley laughed.

"Yeah, I'd like to see that happen." Her mother rolled her eyes. "On second thought, maybe not."

"Thank you," Mia told her father as he held the door open for them. As she stepped inside the lobby, the blast from the air-conditioner hit her like winter wind. She was glad for her jacket. She and Paisley looked around the lobby and spotted a gift shop to the right.

A rack in the shop's window filled with brightly colored dresses and patchwork skirts caught Mia's eye. "Look at the clothes."

"Look at the jewelry," said Paisley, pointing to a case filled with ornate necklaces and earrings.

"Mom, can we—"

Her mother grabbed her shoulders and turned her in the opposite direction. "On the way out."

A man with dark, curly hair and wearing a beige shirt with the same patchwork Mia had noticed on the skirts in the shop approached them with his arm outstretched. "Mr. Bryant?"

"Mr. Emathla?" Mia's father asked, shaking his hand.

"Yes," they replied at the same time and chuckled.

Mr. Emathla smiled. "I'm very pleased to meet you. It's rare that we get to meet an actual descendent of a Black Seminole or Seminole Maroon."

"Black Seminole? Maroon?" Mia whispered to Paisley.

Her mom nudged her. "Shh. . ."

"Thank you for allowing us to stop by even though you're closed for remodeling." Mia's father gestured to his wife. "This is my wife Laura, my daughter Mia, and her friend Paisley."

"Hello, Mia. How old are you? Wait, let me guess." Mr. Emathla rubbed his chin. "About thirteen?"

"No. We're not ready for thirteen," her father said with a laugh. "She's eleven."

"And a half," said Mia. "Paisley too."

"It's a pleasure to meet you both." Mr. Emathla clasped his hands in front of him. "Let me show you around."

Mia nudged her mother. "What's a Black Seminole?"

"You're about to find out," her mother whispered.

They followed Mr. Emathla past dingy white tarps that covered an entire wall.

"What are those for?" Paisley asked.

Mr. Emathla nodded toward the tarps. "Oh, that's a mural. It's almost complete. I can't let you see it right now, but there's going to be a big unveiling next month. Hopefully, you can come back for our grand re-opening."

Mr. Emathla led them through a doorway and then down a hall with a planked floor resembling a boat dock. They turned a corner and entered the first exhibit. Mia stopped in front of a rendering of a river with life-like Indigenous statues.

She lightly touched the canoe, glancing at the sign in front of it. "This was made from a Cypress tree? That's what it says here."

"That's correct," Mr. Emathla replied. "We actually do some canoe carving out back."

"Cool."

Mia nodded as she walked around the room, examining the various artifacts. Much of the exhibit was behind glass, and she was glad because she had an urge to touch everything she saw.

"So, what do you think?" Mr. Emathla asked.

Mia swiveled to face him and shook her head. "I can't believe we've never come here before."

"There's a lot to see, but it's not meant to be seen in one quick pass. This is a very big place." He smiled at her and pointed toward the next exhibit. "I think this will be a good place for you to start."

Mia and Paisley took off around the next corner with Mr. Emathla, then stopped in front of a wall of paintings. A few seconds later, her parents joined them.

Mia gazed at the rendering of a Black Seminole warrior—a girl who appeared to be around her age. She tugged her mother's sleeve. "Mom, look at this. She's beautiful, right?"

Her mother smiled at her husband and pointed at the display.

"This is what we came to show you," her father said proudly. "We are direct descendants of this little girl."

Mia stepped closer to the warrior girl's image. She read the name on the museum label. "Talula. But she was a kid."

"That's correct. And just about your age," said Mr. Emathla. "Would you like to know more about her?"

There was an innocence about Talula, but her dark eyes were so intense that Mia couldn't look away. "Yes."

"She kind of looks like you," said Paisley.

"No, I don't think so. Does she?"

Her mother smiled. "I see it."

Thunder rumbled overhead and the roof rattled. Everyone looked at the ceiling.

Mr. Emathla ran his hand through his curls. "The winds are really picking up out there. You guys chose some day to visit."

"We did, didn't we? See?" Mia nudged her father. She walked ahead to the next painting. "What is Talula doing in this one?"

"Well, that's a long story." Mr. Emathla pointed to a hallway. "But if you'll have a seat in the theater, I would like to show you a little something we have put together for you."

They followed Mr. Emathla to the adjoining room and sat on a white bench on the top row, facing the tall red curtains at the front. The theater was cold and dark. Only a couple of lights shone from the ceiling in front of the curtains.

Mia wiggled in her seat with excitement. "I am dying for a movie!"

"Me too!" said Paisley, wiggling right alongside her. The girls chattered away as they took pictures of the room.

"Let me post it first," said Mia.

Her father nudged her and held a finger to his lips. "Come on now, shh. . . And silence your phones."

Mia covered her mouth and pushed a button on the side of her phone.

"Sorry," both girls whispered.

Mr. Emathla stepped behind the wall behind them and started the projector. The curtains slid open, the screen lit up, and music poured through overhead speakers. Drums, flutes, and native voices filled the air.

Mr. Emathla's smooth deep voice spoke over it. "Have you heard of the underground railroad, Mia?"

"Yes," she exclaimed.

"Here is something you probably didn't know. The underground railroad didn't only run North, it ran south to Spanish Florida. . ."

Mia lifted her chin in surprise. "Spanish Florida? Slaves were free there?"

"Not exactly," Mr. Emathla replied. "Some were given their freedom and land in exchange for military service protecting Florida from Americans. Some were owned by Seminole Indians."

Mia frowned. "But wasn't that the same thing as being enslaved in America?"

"Not at all."

Mia and Paisley exchanged glances, then sat back in their seats as the movie began.

Florida

Year 1812

"'By God, my son will be free.

'Ya here? We are leaving t'night.'

Those were my father's words. I remember them. I sat on the floor of our one room cabin watching Ma and Pa. My father was agitated. It scared me. He was usually a calm man. But behind his eyes, a conversation took place that he was afraid to share. I saw the fear.

I stood there quietly by the stove and watched my parents talk.

'I heard tell slaves are livin' free in their own communities. We can be free.' He pointed at me.

'They are takin' him come morn. I won't let this child be sold. It's the only way.'

Without a word, my mother hurried to fill a cloth with whatever she could carry. She threw it over her shoulder and took my hand.

We left in the dark of the night. As we squatted behind a cabin, my father pulled air into his lungs and whistled. He sounded like a cricket. A moment later, another family emerged from the woods and joined us.

'Which way?' The man asked.

My father turned and jogged away without speaking. Everyone followed him. We journeyed from Georgia, but there were others who came from further away—the Carolinas.

Travel was slow, and I don't know how long we were out there. It was hard. I did not have shoes and my feet swelled and split. At times, my father carried me on his back. We were weak and starving, but our desire to be free fueled our strength to continue on.

'When will we get there?' I asked him over and over again.

'Soon,' he responded each time.

But I didn't believe him. I thought we were to live out our days in a place where land was only mud and water.

'Are you sure you know the way?' I asked.

'Do you feel the sun on this side of your face?' he replied as sweat ran down my face and trickled onto his hand.

'Yes.'

'That's your right side. As long as the sun sets on that side, we are going south. That's the way. But at morn when the sun rises, it should be on the left side of your face until midday.' He tapped me at the center of my forehead. 'That's where the sun is midday.'

One evenin' we stopped for a rest. I'd wandered off. Light flickered and rose and fell in the distance.

I ran back to my father and tugged at his shirt. 'Pa, I hear something.'

'Shh. . . Hush up,' Pa said. All seven of us in our group quieted. They heard it—the horse's hooves.

He turned to my ma. It was too dark to see her eyes, but I knew what she felt. Fear flowed from everyone and surrounded us. I swallowed hard. They could not see the tears that welled in my eyes. No one said the words, but I knew what was happening. Worse than our throbbing feet and hunger. . . the slave hunters were coming.

The sound of horse hooves trotted nearby. I began to speak, but my pa covered my mouth and pushed me into my mother's arms.

'No!' I screamed into her hand.

I was young, but I knew what he was going to do. He would protect his family or die trying.

'Get them out to freedom,' he told another man who was with us. My pa hugged me hard and kissed my face. 'Be good for your ma, hear?'

'No,' I cried into Ma's hand.

But I knew my pa. He was strong. He would stare down the devil himself and say, 'You will not have me, suh.' And his voice would be filled with enough power that the devil would leave him be.

Now, he placed a leather rope that he wore around my neck. I never saw him without it. 'Remember Africa,' he told me.

'But you never seen Africa.'

He was my Africa. The sound of it, the smell, the soil. I knew it 'cause I knew him. I hear the drums since that day. They carried me away to this place and call to my soul.

My pa motioned at my ma. 'She can read. You need her.'

'Come,' the other man said. I believe his name was George.

'No matter what you hear, do not stop running. Freedom is waiting for you,' Pa told me.

They dragged me away. My father and the father of the other family nodded at each other, and the two of them turned back. Their plan was to draw the slave hunters away.

T'was the last time I saw him.

The next day, we hid while my Ma ran to read the words on a house with a wooden cross on the door. She knocked and didn't have to say anything. The man who opened the door told us to get into his wagon. He drove us a long ways and let us off. I remember his words. 'God be with you.'"

"What happened next?" Talula yelled from the top floor of a palmetto thatch-roofed cabin.

"You've heard this story a hundred times, Talula. Rest now," her father yelled back.

All of the children listened as the adults told stories by the fire each night until they fell asleep. Talula's father's former life of slavery was unknown to her. She hugged her doll and closed her eyes, happy she'd known nothing but peace. She thanked the Breathmaker and drifted off to sleep.

The last thing she remembered hearing was, "How did you know when you made it? Did you find other slaves?"

"No, they found us."

"Who?"

"Seminoles."

Chapter Two

Talula awoke to the smell of the morning meal cooking outside over an open fire. Her mother and the other women of the village were already up and working as they did each day. Ma didn't wake her at first light to teach her the ways of Seminole women as she usually did. That meant something was wrong. But Talula didn't hear the muffled voices of a meeting or horses or anyone yelling of drought and the condition of the crops.

She rolled over, not ready to open her eyes yet. She had dreamed of the people in her settlement running. Smoke and flames had shot up around them in the brush. An old man had carried a child. "Lat-kus!" he'd shouted, telling her to run. And she had. Then she'd seen her ma looking back at her, and her pa behind her telling her to go. But she couldn't see why or what it was behind them that caused such a fright. Instead of following her ma, she'd run back to her father. In an instant, everyone had disappeared, and she'd stood alone. A dragonfly flitted over her head, and she'd followed it, laughing and running through a wet field of string lilies. After that, Talula awoke. In the end, it was a pleasant dream.

She opened her eyes, seeing black, and yelped. Her long strands of thick wavy hair covered her face and lay trapped beneath her.

Talula's hair was dark brown, not like her ma's. Ma's was darker than the blackness of night and stick-straight. Like the other Seminole women, she had bangs and wore her locks in a high bun. But because Talula wasn't pure Seminole, she didn't have to wear the customary hairstyle. Yet. Although they lived in a Black Seminole village instead of with her mother's clan, they still followed the rules of the Seminole micco. Talula had been named in the tradition of her Seminole side by her grandmother. Talula—one who leaps water.

Now, she sat up and pulled her hair back, then rolled up her bed of hides and the blanket her pa traded for. She took her Seminole dress and three glass bead necklaces from a basket beside her bed and put them on. From the rafters above her head hung a box that contained her favorite treasures—a ball, some shells, and a doll. She started to reach for it but instead, climbed down to the lower floor of their cabin, slid her bare feet into her moccasins, and went outside looking for her father.

The sun was coming up, and her eyes tightened against the light.

She spotted her mother at the fire, pounding away at zamia roots and stems, preparing coontie flour. Talula was supposed to be beside her, learning to leach the poison from the plant to make it edible. A pan of sofkee cooked above the fire on an iron grate over logs arranged like the spokes of a wheel. As they burned, the logs only needed to be pushed in toward the center to keep the fire going.

During the day, Talula worked alongside Ma, making baskets from palmetto leaves and sweetgrass, cooking, or working in the fields. All the girls did. The boys worked alongside the men, either with the herds of livestock, fishing, or building. There were some who worked with the crops too.

As Talula approached her, Ma looked up, but Talula ducked behind the cabin. Talula often wished she was a boy so she could spend the day fishing or hunting or building. Those things seemed more fun, though when she pictured the innocent eyes of a fawn, she couldn't imagine hunting deer. She occasionally accompanied her pa while he tended the cattle, but for only short periods.

Though her mouth watered for fry bread, Talula hurried behind the cabins and passed the central cookhouse, where the elders prepared the midday meals. She ducked beside a post and listened to the woman who sang there every morning. Children often gathered around to listen to her sing to her child in an African language. She once told Talula that she sang of her child's freedom. Of him being free to run, swim, and sore like the eagle. The child's name was ❖ Juan Caballo. His father was a Seminole trader.

Talula stepped from behind the post and hummed along as she walked by. The woman grinned at her as the baby lay nuzzled against her.

Once outside her village, Talula knelt every few feet and examined the earth. A grin covered her face. "There it is." She found a raised edge of soil shaped like a horseshoe.

She straightened and ran, following the young voices coming from the direction of the river. Ben, Abraham, Oscar, and Eneah (any-ah) stood along the bank, holding bows.

Talula crouched in the long grass, then lowered her voice as deep as she could and bellowed, "Mooooo-oarrrr!"

The boys searched the grass around them with their gazes, preparing to run.

Talula shot up, laughing.

Ben waved her off. "Look who is here, again."

Talula grinned. "You thought I was an alligator."

"No we didn't," said Ben with his chest heaving. He turned to his friends. "How did she find us this time?"

Talula pointed at the horse tied to a nearby tree. "They are easier to track."

Ben glared at Oscar. "I told you to walk like the rest of us."

She moved closer to see what they were doing, and Abraham pushed her away.

"You are a girl, ain't ya? Go back to your woman chores."

"I am not a woman yet. I can do as I want," said Talula. She picked up one of their bows and an arrow.

"What is she fix'n to do?" asked Oscar.

"Let her try," said Eneah, who was part Seminole like Talula.

She examined the bow in her hands. "The men use muskets."

Ben scowled at her. "No. Muskets scare the deer away. We hunt with bows."

"We know how to make bows, do you?" asked Abraham, as if even the thought of Talula working with tools was silly.

"I can learn." Talula nocked the arrow, then aimed it at a tree in the opposite direction, pulled it back, and released it. The arrow didn't hit the tree, nor did it go more than a few feet.

The boys snorted with laughter.

"Go and carve your bowls," said Abraham.

"You must remember the arrow is not a weapon," Eneah told her. "It is a tool. It becomes part of you. It is an extension of the hand and arm and shoulder and back." He patted her shoulder.

Talula picked up another arrow and nocked it, then pulled it and aimed at the tree again.

Eneah gently pushed her elbow up. "Pull straight back along the side of your face."

Talula shot again, but the arrow landed only a few inches further than the last one.

Eneah patted his stomach. "Tight. Here." He bent over and pulled at her moccasin, moving her feet further apart. "There."

The other boys laughed again, sneering at her.

Ben put his hands on his hips. "Is ya leavin' or ain't ya?"

Talula lifted her chin. "I ain't."

She was disappointed the arrow hadn't gone far, but she tried not to show it as she readied another arrow.

"You can keep this one," said Eneah, tapping the bow in her hands.

From that day on, whenever Talula snuck away from her daily chores, she practiced with the bow Eneah had given her. She kept it tied to a branch in an oak tree near the river, so her mother wouldn't find it.

She often hid and watched the boys from a distance. They'd all played together when they were younger, before they had so many chores. But they acted like they were already men now.

"If I did not have to wear this skirt, I could run as fast as them," she told herself.

One morning, Talula knelt, examining the earth, and found three tiny white crumbs. The boys tried to trick her, but she'd found them because of Oscar. He ate more often than the others. And this time, since Talula was so clever in finding them, the boys didn't argue when she interfered. But they chuckled when she did no better with the bow and arrows than the last time.

As Eneah handed Talula an arrow, her father's whistle pierced the air. She hurried back to their village.

As she ran up to the fire, her mother caught her by the arm. "Talula, you cannot run away the way you do. There are chores and your lessons. Your father searches for you."

Talula lowered her eyes. "I am sorry."

"Go to him, now."

Despite the heat of the day, a light breeze blew through the air. Talula ran faster through the rich earth, stirring up the gnats and bugs on the plant life. She found her father near the river. Jacob was the name given to him on the plantation, but he said his pa called him by another name—Kofi, after his grandfather. He stood taller than most in the village. The scar above his eyes came from a day when he'd helped Seminole Indians and other Black Seminoles defend their land from settlers.

His dark, smooth skin sparkled with sweat. Unlike some of the other adults in their village, he didn't have a letter or symbol branded on his back, chest, or arm.

He reached into the slowly moving water and cupped his hands, then splashed it on his face. After wiping his hands together, he glanced at her.

"There you are, Talula. Are you ready for your lesson?" he asked. "Although, I believe you've already had one."

The sly grin on his face told Talula that he must have watched her shooting the bow with the boys from afar.

She kicked at the dirt. "Why can't I do boy chores?"

"Because you are female, and you know your place. Now, pay attention."

He used a stick to write a word in English in the moist soil. Talula had been taught to read the

English language just like Pa's mother had taught him.

She read the word aloud. "Dog."

"Good," her father said. Then he drew a picture of an animal. "What is that?"

"Squirrel."

"Spell it."

She sounded it out. "Sss. . . S. Ssk. K."

Pa shook his head. "No."

She furrowed her brow, thinking. "S. C. W."

"No," he replied again. "Queen, Quest. I have taught you this."

Frustration mounted inside Talula. "Tell me."

"No."

He put his hands on his hips, and Talula got nervous. He was stern about her lessons, often carrying a thin branch to swat at her hands. If she didn't pay attention, *whack*.

"Skwa. . ." Her brows rose. "It is S. Q. U."

"That is right." He wrote out the word for her. "I know you think I am hard on you, but your lessons are very important for your future."

"Why am I the only one who knows how to read?"

Jacob thought for a moment, and then nodded. "One day soon, we will have lessons for all."

Talula grinned, and they finished her lesson with more animal words. After they were done, she took her father's hand as they walked back to the village.

"We have fine crops and cattle. Maybe we can trade for a book from one of the other settlements," Jacob told her.

Talula hugged him tight. "Do you think they have one?"

"It is worth finding out."

"And sugar cane?" Talula asked excitedly.

"Hmmm. . ." Her father rubbed his chin. "Perhaps."

The next day, Talula woke at first light. She donned her dress and her strings of beads, then left their cabin to go about her chores just as she was supposed to.

She stayed close to her mother, listening to her gentle talk of the old ways. As soft spoken as her mother was, she was strong in spirit. Talula had seen her spirit before when the rains came, and it seemed like they would never stop. She took care of everyone in the village, the wounded and the ill, and shared all she had so no one went without.

As she worked, Talula thought back on what her father had said about trading some of their wares for a book. The idea of having a book of her own made Talula want to work even harder to please her parents. She didn't search out the boys that day or climb the oak tree to get her bow.

During her free time, she chased butterflies and dragonflies. She laid in the field and listened to the wind and the birds in the trees. She watched squirrels chasing each other. She was at peace and happy.

But that happiness left her when a little boy appeared in the woods alongside the field. He was naked, running through the trees, with skin like her father's.

Chapter Three

Talula knelt behind an oak tree and watched the boy, her heart pounding. The boy, covered in dried mud, couldn't have been more than three years old. She crept closer to him, not wanting to scare him. Jacob would not be happy she had followed the child. He had warned her before that her curiosity would get her in trouble, much like the time she'd come too close to an alligator. He'd said she should've gone home and told an adult it was nearby. But this boy was no alligator, and he might need her help.

Talula looked toward the village, then turned back toward the boy. Where was he going? And where had he come from? He took off running again, and she pushed her way after him through the limbs of the forest trees.

Someone called out, and then a man came out through the trees and scooped him up. Three more adults emerged and joined them. Their clothes were dirty and worn. The woman looked frail, like she might be ill. They all held fear in their eyes like Talula had never seen before.

They began to head in the other direction. Talula hurried through the brush behind them. Suddenly, they stopped and moved so they stood back-to-back with their arms extended, except for the man who carried the boy.

A turban with a feather attached appeared above the bushes, then came out in the open to reveal a man cutting off the group's path.

"He's a Seminole warrior," Talula said to herself. More Seminoles dotted the area surrounding them. They held bows and arrows pointed at the family. Talula froze.

The man struggled with the boy, who kicked to be put down.

"We mean no harm." His voice trembled. "We mean no harm, I say. Please let us pass. We have no weapons."

The warriors didn't move. They watched the fearful group as if they were waiting for something more.

Talula leaned her back against the oak tree, fighting within herself. She was not to interfere in these matters. Jacob would scold her.

Her gaze caught on a warrior suddenly standing in front of her, and he wasn't alone. More warriors appeared in the trees, surrounding her. But she wasn't afraid.

"Istonko," she said. The closest warrior only stared at her, and she wished she hadn't greeted him.

"They do not understand you," she yelled to the cowering people.

Finally, she revealed her full body, stepping from behind the tree.

She looked to the warriors' leader and spoke to him in the Seminole language. "I can interpret."

He nodded at her, then asked in his language if there were more people hiding in the woods.

She turned to the man holding the squirming boy. "He asks if there are more of you."

The man shook his head, struggling to hold the boy still. "No."

The warrior leader spoke again. "Cimarron."

"What is he saying?" one of the women asked, her eyes still wide with fear.

"Runaway," said Talula.

The warrior spoke again, and Talula nodded.

"He wants you to follow them," she told the group.

As quickly as they had arrived, the Seminoles disappeared into the woods.

The exhausted-looking group of people didn't move.

"We don't mean no harm," the man said again, still clutching the child.

"Leave us be," the woman called out, wringing her hands.

"We beg you," he added.

The woman pulled at his arm. "We cannot defend ourselves."

"You do not have to defend yourselves from us," Talula told them.

The man, his body shaking and his eyes darting in every direction, asked, "Where are we going?"

"To our village. It is okay," said Talula. "My pa is there. He is like you."

The man's eyes widened.

Talula began to walk toward home, then glanced over her shoulder and waved for them to follow.

The man glanced at his group, then began to follow her.

They soon arrived at Talula's village, which was bustling with activity. People walking by with baskets, leading horses, or just going from one place to another, stopped what they were doing and watched the Seminoles emerging from the forest.

"I told you," the man behind Talula told his companions. "A village of slaves and freedmen."

His voice shook, and Talula thought he might scream with excitement because of how his pitch raised.

"Just like Mr. Gaines told Master Charles. 'The finest looking people I have ever seen. Strong and intelligent.'"

Jacob appeared in the crowd, then hurried over to them with concern etched on his face.

The woman began to cry, hiding her face with her hands.

"Don't worry. You are safe now," Jacob told her in a soothing voice. "Talula, what is this? Why are you with these people?"

"I was their interpreter," she said with a grin.

Jacob's gaze darted from Talula to the Seminoles, and then to the runaway slaves. He glanced to the ground and back to their faces. He looked concerned, but Talula didn't know why.

"I was near the fields," Talula told him. "They came from that way."

"The swamp rice fields?"

"No, Pa. The corn fields."

Jacob looked in that direction. "Get to your ma." He went over to the Seminoles and lowered his voice as he spoke to them. Then, the Seminoles set off in a hurried jog.

Talula's mother joined them, putting her arm around Talula's shoulder.

"Bring water and sofkee," her father told a boy nearby. Then he whistled and circled his hand. All the village men stopped what they were doing or left their cabins, then hurried away in different directions.

The boy returned with a friend, both of them carrying bowls filled with water for the runaways.

The group cried out in thanks and drank heartily.

"What are they doing? Where are they going?" Talula asked her mother of the men that left the village.

"Nothing a child needs to know," she replied and watched the group.

"Where did you come from?" Jacob asked the man holding the bowl of water to the little boy's mouth. "Carolina, Georgia?"

"Yes, suh. Carolina," the man said, while coughing from the water. His hands shook as he passed the bowl to the man beside him.

"Rice farmers?" Jacob asked.

"Yes, suh," all four of the adults replied.

A young girl rushed up to the runaways with clean garments and blankets. They took them gratefully.

"You bathe," said Talula's mother. "Come."

They followed her but stayed close together, as if they weren't certain if they were safe.

"Why are they so afraid," asked Talula.

Her father watched them leaving. "They're not used to being free."

The man holding the boy looked over his shoulder. "Thank you, suh."

Jacob raised his hand. "Jacob. Call me Jacob."

That evening, the settlement's elders gathered together at the center of the village as the newcomers rested in a cabin.

Talula circled the crowd and tried to squeeze between the adults to hear what they were saying.

Her mother called to her from their cabin door. But Talula kept asking, "What has happened? Why is everyone upset?"

The elders talked as if she wasn't there.

"They runnin'. Coming in from the north and west. No one is safe. Not you, you, or you!" A man named Tandy pointed at people as he spoke.

Talula stood on her tiptoes, trying to see around the people in front of her. "Who are they?" she asked.

"The hunters will come to take us back," said another man.

"I'm a free man," said another.

"The slave hunters do not care about slave or free. They only know the color of your skin. And our children's skin," said Tandy.

Talula found her father standing near Tandy and pulled his hand. "Pa."

Jacob looked down at her, pulled his hand from her grasp and waved, trying to shoo her away. "We are meeting with the micco at the talwa tonight," he told the group.

"We are?" asked Talula.

Tandy sucked his teeth and motioned at Jacob. "This is no place for a child. And she helped lead them here."

Jacob stiffened. "Keep my child out of it. They made it here just like other runaway slaves have tried. Just like you did. Or have you forgotten how you came from Alabama?"

"This is not the underground railroad," Tandy whispered loudly, pointing at the cabin the newcomers slept in.

"Yes, it is." With each word, Jacob seemed to rise taller over the elder. "Who are you to determine who should make it to freedom and who shouldn't?"

Someone pulled Talula's arm. She was certain it was her mother but turned to find her friend ❖ William Powell. Everyone called him Billy. He'd been trying to hear what was being said. If Talula was a Black Seminole, he was a White. His father was British, but he had never met him. His mother, Polly, was Creek and Scottish. He and his mother had come to Florida a few years before. Now, he was eight years old and 'already showing promise as a leader,' as she had heard one of the elders say. All of the other boys listened to him.

She and Billy walked away from the elders. Billy called together the village children who formed their own circle just outside the elders, mimicking them.

"We will follow them tonight," said Billy. "To the micco."

Talula's stomach clenched. "Pa will not like that."

Billy crossed his arms. "Do you think about what your pa will not like when you follow us boys to the river? We are only a short distance from the talwa. They will not tell us what they fear or what the chief will say, so we will go and see for ourselves."

Abraham puffed his chest. "The girls can stay here. We are not taking them."

"We go together," said Billy, who didn't care that Talula was a girl and often let her in on whatever he was doing. She appreciated that.

Fear spread over the adults like the spray of a skunk and hovered over the village. It felt so thick that Talula was sure if she looked up, she'd see a smoky mist. If the children didn't get away from the adults soon, the fear would engulf them too.

"No, the Seminole warriors will see us coming," said Oscar. "And if we get caught, 'tis a whopping for all of us."

A cracking sound filled the air, causing everyone to look up in alarm.

"Was that thunder?" Ben asked.

Billy frowned. "No. It was a musket."

At the elders' circle, a young African man named Amos ran up to Jacob. Talula loved to hear him speak. He had a different accent than the others.

He pointed into the distance. "It is near, from the next village."

"Are you sure?" asked Jacob.

"Yes."

"Get the men together."

"See, we get the *men* together," Abraham jeered at Talula.

After more men gathered, Talula stayed close, trying to hear what they looked so concerned about. After some tense discussion, her father and nine other men jogged off into the darkness, carrying muskets.

Talula had a hard time sleeping that night. All was quiet, but her anxious mind kept her awake. When the silence was broken by her neighbors' voices in the cabin next door, she got up and hurried downstairs from her loft.

She was surprised to see her father was back. He stood in the doorway watching the commotion outside.

She joined him and saw families loading their belongings and walking by, huddled together. "Pa, people are leaving. Going south. Are we leaving?"

His jaw clenched. "I have been here since I was a boy. This is our home. We are not going anywhere."

Talula shifted nervously. "But they say bad men are coming."

"Who told you that? Billy?"

"Yes. They say they can go to the tribes."

"We are not the same as the people of the tribes. You are." He glanced at her. "But you are also me."

"Why are we not the same?"

Jacob sighed. "You know this, Talula. Your mother is Seminole."

Talula frowned. "I am Black."

"Because you are born to a Seminole mother, you are part of her tribe. Had your mother been Black and your father Seminole, you would not be."

"But you said we are Black Seminoles."

He nodded, leaning against the doorway. "Yes, we have adopted the Seminole customs. We live among them but in our own villages. They gave us tools to build our own cabins, and we raise our own crops, like the maize we bring to your uncle as tribute."

"But you are a translator," Talula insisted.

"Yes, and I am needed by the neighboring villages and settlements. I speak the language of the White man, of the Spanish, and of the Seminoles. They need me."

"I speak those languages, too."

"That is right, you do." He gave her a slight smile. "And a little my father taught me from Africa. Sleep now, Talula." He took her elbow and led her to the loft ladder.

She pulled away from him, not wanting to go back to bed yet. "Tell me about Africa."

"I only know what my father told me," he replied. "I do not know if he saw Africa with his own eyes. We had different chores on the plantation. I worked in the cotton fields, but at the end of the day, we came together. While he pressed a poultice into my hands, which was made from the plants of a necklace of seeds brought from Africa and worn as a protective amulet during travel in the slave vessel—"

"Tell me about the vessel."

He raised a brow. "I thought you wanted to know about Africa."

She leaned into his side. "I forgot."

He put his arm around her. "You will never understand its simplicity, beauty, or strength."

"As beautiful as our land?" She craned her neck to look up at him.

His eyes grew misty. "More beautiful."

"But you did not go to Africa."

"No. I did not." Jacob tugged at the leather rope around his neck.

Talula looked out the window at the sky. "I wonder if Africa's sky has as many stars as ours, or if there is a little girl there who has never seen a dragonfly?"

"There are dragonflies in Africa too."

"There are? I want to see. Can we go there?"

"Jacob," someone called from outside. Her pa patted her back, urging her to climb up to her loft. "Rest now, little one. I will come back soon."

He left her and went outside to greet whoever had called his name.

Talula pretended to go up to her loft, but then went and leaned against the wall beside the door.

The man's voice sounded strained. "I've been to Payne's town and the neighboring villages. It is true, the Patriots are coming to seize our lands."

"Thank you, friend," said Jacob.

"What are you going to do?"

"Speak with the Seminoles."

Jacob was distracted. He hadn't been himself since Talula and the Seminole warriors had delivered the escaped slaves to the settlement. He sat on the wooden chair in their living area with his face drawn and brows knit together.

Talula approached him. "Pa, what is wrong?"

"The drums have stopped."

"The African drums from your father?" She remembered the story he'd told by the fireside.

Jacob didn't respond. He pulled at the leather rope around his neck, turning it side to side.

For Talula and her village, their whole world changed that day. Talula said goodbye to most of her friends. The adults attended many meetings and traveled to meet with other tribes, and her father went with them as a translator. They carried word that the Americans' imminent war with England had begun. ❖

With so many people gone, Talula helped with some of the boys' chores and tended to the livestock as her father would. Against her mother's will, she even dressed like the boys so she could easily run. She wore a tunic and leggings that Eneah had given her.

She spent her little free time roaming through the elms and cypresses, learning her way through the forest. She went a greater distance each day.

One day while on her way to the river, the ground trembled beneath Talula's feet. She followed her first instinct, which was to stoop and lower herself in the grass.

A man ran through the nearby thicket, flailing his arms.

Talula's chest tightened. "Another slave."

She began to stand, but the sound of galloping horses made her duck back into the grass. What must have been a dozen riders came tearing out of the trees. One flung a rope through the air and it landed over the runaway's head, snatching him backwards. He grasped desperately at his neck.

"We got him," the rider hollered to his comrades.

Another man removed the rope. "Chain him up."

"You escaped from a plantation, didn't you?"

"No'sa!" the man said.

"Then why did you run? Show me your papers."

"I was a free man before I came here!"

Talula couldn't see all of the hunters' faces, but she noticed that some were Indians, but not Seminoles. They weren't dressed like Seminoles.

One of the riders with his back to her said, "You can't prove it, so you're coming with me."

"Look, grab the boy!" One of the riders pointed to a boy crouching in the grass across from Talula.

The closest man shot off on his horse to catch the child. He jumped off and snatched the small boy and dragged him to the river.

"No!" the man on the ground shrieked in tears.

Talula's heart pounded as she scrambled to the water, careful to stay quiet and out of sight.

The hunter lifted the boy, who squirmed in his arms. "You like to run? Now let's see if you can swim!"

He hurled the boy into the river. The boy sank down, his arms and legs flailing, weighted down by the water. As it flowed over his face, Talula saw the terror in his eyes. The man squatted, watching the poor child, then stood, his arms folded across his chest.

"We just gonna leave him?" asked a man who joined him

Talula lowered her voice and bellowed, "Mooooo-oarrrr!"

"There's a patch of alligators in there!" He jumped back, then hurried to his horse.

Talula's mind reeled. She didn't fully understand what she had just seen. *Why would they harm a child?* she wondered.

Once she was sure she was out of their sight, she hurried and slid down to the water's edge. It turned out the boy could swim, but he hadn't shown it while the hunters were watching. He crawled out of the river, gasping. Talula hurried to him, still in a crouched position to avoid detection.

She wanted to tell the boy that he didn't do anything wrong and that the men were evil. That everything would be okay. She glanced over her shoulder towards the men, who were paying the river no attention, then stood and slowly walked toward the boy. As she got closer, her stride became faster. Her heart beat wildly in her chest. When she got close to him, she held her hands up so he wouldn't be frightened.

"I saw," she said and pointed to the long grass near the bank. "Go to that grass and lay down and wait."

He nodded at her and did as she said. He slipped into the foliage and out of sight.

Talula inched up the bank, closer to the hunters.

"He can lead us to more of them," one of them said.

"Did you see their fields?" another replied. "The Black Indians are intelligent, and they speak English, Indian, and Spanish. These towns are full of escaped slaves, and they protect the Indians. I want that land."

"The Spanish governor has proclaimed freedom to every negro who joins his army," the first man replied. "It won't be easy."

"Stay on alert. Go back the way he came. There may be more that we missed."

Talula stayed low and watched. A wagon had joined them, and the man they'd just roped now sat inside it with a dozen or so women and children. The hunters took off with their prisoners. When they were out of sight, Talula went to the boy and took his hand. They hurried back to her village, shaking. When she saw the light of their fire burning in the distance, she couldn't hold it in any longer and screamed for her father as she ran with the boy.

"Talula," Jacob said, catching her by the arms. He glanced at the boy, who stood by, watching them. "What has happened?"

She was out of breath. "I saw them," she said, taking a breath between each word. "I followed them." She cried. Her pulse thudded in her throat. "They were taking our people in a wagon cage." She pointed in the direction they'd come from. "They were taking them in a wagon," she repeated, trembling.

The boy nodded, tears welling in his eyes. "My pa."

"Who?" asked Jacob, his voice hoarse.

"The Patriots," Talula replied.

Jacob's eyes widened. "How do you know this word, Patriots?"

"I heard someone say it."

"What else did you hear, child?"

Talula didn't want to say. She would have to tell that she and Billy had spied on their meeting to find out what was happening.

"Tell me," her father insisted.

She avoided his gaze. "Battles to the north. Fleeing villages. Seminoles and Blacks cutting off their supply paths."

Her father released her. "Go to your ma. Take the boy with you."

He whistled, calling everyone in the village to him.

Talula took the boy's hand again and led him to her ma at their cabin. Things were changing, too much and too fast for her. Her peaceful village was now filled with what she'd never seen before—fear, hate, and war. She wondered if this was the reason that Jacob's drumming had stopped.

Seminole scouts told her pa that the hunters were from Georgia. They were rounding up those who looked like former slaves.

A few days later, Talula found her family rushing around their cabin, packing everything in sight.

Smoke rose in the distance outside, and Talula sprinted from the cabin and ran toward it. Jacob ran after her and seized her by the shoulder.

He looked at her gravely. "Do not dress like the other settlers anymore. Do you hear?"

"Why?"

"If the slave hunters find you, they will take you," he said. "Wear your Seminole dress and beads like your mother. You are not a Black Seminole. Only speak the Seminole language."

"But—"

Her father squeezed her shoulder. "You don't know what it is like to be owned by another man. It's not the same, like what we have with the Seminoles."

"But—"

"Do as you are told."

Talula went back inside and changed into the long skirt and short blouse her mother had made for her, then went back out to her father.

Jacob yelled, frightening her. "What clan are you from? Who is your chief?"

Talula responded in the Creek language.

"Good. You were afraid but answered correctly."
He hugged her. "Talula, you must go. It is not safe
here anymore."

She hugged him back. "Then you must come
too."

"No, I have to stay here and help." He kissed the
top of her head. "Go with your ma. I will find you."

Talula and her mother left immediately and met up
with other Seminoles that were leaving the area.
There was no time to gather anything other than
tools, blankets, food, and seeds for planting. Talula
had scrambled up to her loft before leaving and had
taken her doll from the box tied to the rafter. Once
outside, she turned and ran back in to get a book of
her father's—the only book he owned.

On their journey, the forest was thick with
branches and roots with no paths cleared. Most of
the time, they walked in murky water. Talula
longed for the bed of her cabin. Some of the
villagers were old and traveling was hard. There
was no place dry to build a fire, so they kept going
for hours and hours. It reminded Talula of the
stories her pa told of him and his mother escaping
to Florida.

After hours of trudging through the wet wilderness, a young woman traveling with them started to cry. "I cannot go any further."

Talula's mother silenced her. "You can."

It was the most assertive Talula had ever heard her.

Her ma bent over to look the girl in the eyes. "Do not think of all the steps you must take. Focus on one step, and then the next."

The girl nodded, and Talula's mother took her by the hand and helped her continue on.

With every crack of a branch or rustle of leaves, Talula thought the slave hunters had found them. She'd never seen a White man close up and imagined them to be as white as the white feathers of a great egret. She worried the hunters would capture the whole village and sell them all into slavery.

But that was the least of her mother's concerns. When they stopped for a rest, her mother looked around for supplies. "It has not rained, and we need clean water and food."

"We will find it," Talula assured her.

A day later, they reached high ground. They found a clearing, and the Seminoles said good spirits were there, so it was a good place to build their chickees.

Talula's mother walked with her to the back of the area. They were Black Seminoles and didn't live among the Indians. They watched as the Seminoles performed ceremonies to bless the land.

Not far off, the other Black Seminoles came together and set up their camp. They chopped down some trees to build chickees, and the women and children gathered palms for the palmetto thatching of the roofs.

After a few days, they had a decent dwelling. When her mother was fed, settled, and resting, Talula rose, careful not to wake her, and then packed her sack and departed the new settlement. She stopped at a river, remembering the story of her father traveling to Florida, and what his father did to save him. She feared her father was somewhere near their old village fighting to keep them free just as his father had.

Chapter Four

A dragonfly buzzed around Talula's head.

"Am I going the right way?" she asked it.

It flew high above, flitting to the nearest tree.

"You are right. I must go higher." Talula climbed the tree. From there, she could see what was ahead of her.

A creek trickled nearby. She always felt best near water. It was like something was wrong within her being if she wasn't. She didn't have to see it. She only had to know it was near. A river, a spring, or a lake. Like it was part of her.

She peered further, looking for the sign of smoke from someone's camp, a flag, horses, or men. Jacob was out there somewhere.

Below her, the shrubs shook.

"I can see you," Talula said, peering at the forest floor.

She climbed down the tree and jumped off a lower branch. A Black boy with no pants stepped out of the bushes. His hair was short and matted. He wore a long dirty shirt and shoes that were too large for him.

Talula pointed at herself. "Good evenin'. I am Talula." That's how she thought her pa would've introduced himself.

The boy looked afraid to run, yet maybe afraid not to.

"Where are your pants?" she asked. The sharp edges of saw grass were sure to have caused the cuts on his bare legs.

"Ain't got none," the boy replied. "I's Tip."

"What you doing here, Tip? You by yourself?"

"You talk like us."

"Yes, how did you think I would speak?"

He tilted his head. "Like Indians."

"Me and my pa are translators," she replied. "We speak many languages. Where are your kin?"

"The hunters took them back to the plantation."

"Shh. . ." came from behind him.

"I ain't said nothin' but the truth," Tip yelled toward the field on the other side of the trees.

Talula looked toward the field and back at Tip. His stomach growled, sounding like an animal ready to attack.

Talula held her sack tightly. She needed enough food to make it back, but the boy needed it more. She tossed him a piece of fry bread. "Here, eat this."

Tip's eyes widened, and he grabbed the food hastily. Then he turned and waved. A girl rose from the grass several feet behind him. She was taller than him and had a braid on each side of her head and one in back, and she wore a shirt like Tip's.

"Hurry up, Mae," Tip told her, then he took a bite and looked at Talula. "Your kin gone too?"

"Yes." Talula reached in her satchel for a piece of fry bread for Mae.

Mae began to scratch her calves.

"Leave it be." Tip pointed at the bug bites on Mae's legs. "You will make it worse."

"They took your ma and pa?" asked Talula.

"Yes'um. We's by ourself," Mae whimpered.

"Me too." said Talula.

"The hunters took your'n too?" Tip asked.

"No." Talula looked away, suddenly ashamed of herself for leaving her mother when theirs had been taken. "How did you get away?"

Tip swallowed. "Pa hid us."

"Told us not to come out," said Mae. "Told us to shut our eyes and cover our ears."

Talula stared at them. "Did you see what happened? Did you hear?"

"Yes'um." Tip gazed at his feet. "Muskets and screams."

"I hugged my brother, and we stayed there with critters crawl'n all around," May said quietly. "We never came out. Even when it gone quiet."

Talula's throat thickened. "You are out now."

"Cause we came out at night," Tip said. "Everybody was gone."

"Were you here?" Talula asked.

Tip shrugged. "Where is here?"

"Florida."

Tip and Mae looked at each other. "We free?"

Talula wasn't sure, she could only go by her father's stories. His family had fled the plantation to Florida for freedom. Others came because the Spanish had promised them freedom.

"Yes," Talula said and grinned. Though she expected the boy and girl to leap for joy, they didn't. How could they? Their parents were taken by the slave hunters.

Talula slung her bag's strap over her shoulder. "I must be on my way."

"Where you going?" asked Tip.

Talula pointed behind them.

He shook his head. "No, do not go that way. They gon' get you."

But that was the way Talula had to go, toward their village. She was sure her father was there, maybe in a cage waiting to be rescued.

"Where are *you* going?" Talula asked.

Mae began to cry. "We don't know."

Talula felt so sad for them. She couldn't imagine what she would do without her parents, left to wander, looking for food and shelter and afraid of everyone.

"Follow me," she said. "I know these woods."

She'd left to find her father, but she couldn't leave Tip and Mae out there alone. And it was dangerous to take them with her. The only thing she could do was take them to her new home.

They were careful as they traveled through the brush. Something slithered through the grass in front of them, and Talula stopped and held her arm out.

"Snake."

The siblings jumped behind her.

She gave them a knowing look. "It is well that you can see it. Beware of the snakes that hide. They have poison."

The siblings nodded and carefully stepped over the area the snake had crossed.

They walked for half a day. Tip had lots to say, telling Talula about all the things she never knew about slavery. Frightening things that were sure to return to her in her dreams.

To Tip's irritation, she found herself asking over and over, "Why would they do that?"

"I don't know," he answered every time.

"I'm thirsty," said Talula.

"Me too," said Tip.

"Because you won't stop talking," Mae fussed.

They were quiet after that, and Talula walked faster. Tip and Mae hurried after her. It was almost dusk when she neared her new home.

"Talula!" Her mother ran to her and held her tight.

Jacob stepped out from their dwelling, and Talula's heart leapt. "Pa!" she screamed, then ran to him and held his neck as he squatted to her level.

Her mother crossed her arms. "Where did you go?"

Talula's stomach lurched, and she pointed at the kids walking up behind her. "I—I helped Tip and Mae. Their family is gone." She thought it a good excuse that would pacify her parents until later.

Jacob beckoned to them. "Come."

Tip and Mae's faces brightened.

Talula's mother and some other women brought the new children food and water. As Tip and Mae ate, they told everyone about their journey. Afterwards, Ma saw to their injuries and gave them a place to lay in their family's chickee.

Their new home was different from the cabin. The top was thatched palmetto leaves, and the sides were open to the outside. They slept in one chickee and ate in another.

"It is easy to break down and put back up," Ma had told Talula while they were building it. "If we have to leave."

It didn't protect them from the cold wind and blowing rain, but at least they had shelter.

Something was awry in the new village. Each day, Black Seminoles arrived from other settlements, but Talula could see they hadn't left in a hurry like the people from her village had. They arrived with horses, cattle, and mules with sacks strapped to them. The men went about building chickees for the newcomers. Ma helped the women get settled, and Talula assisted the children.

dulichia

She joined a group that were at the base of a hill. One of them walked past his friends with his body as stiff as a board, kicking his feet out. He carried a stick against his shoulder as if it were a musket. "I have seen them; this is how they walk."

"Who?" asked Talula.

"The British soldiers," he replied. "And they wear coats so red you can see them coming through the trees from a long distance away."

"They promised us protection from the Americans, but where are they?" Talula asked. "Where are the Spanish?"

"They are at war," said the boy Talula had found at the river.

Talula's mother and father caught her attention. They stood a little ways away in a serious conversation. She quietly went and stood behind them so she could hear, hoping they wouldn't notice her.

"She has to go with me," said Jacob.

"No," Ma said. She spoke to him in broken English. "She not woman. She must stay."

Tip went running by toward Mae, holding a green fruit in each hand. "They have apples!"

Talula ran over and snatched them away.

"Those are mine," said Tip.

Talula held them behind her back. "Pond apples. The seeds are poison. You cannot eat everything you see. You must ask."

"They are?" asked Mae.

"Yes. I will show you."

Jacob saw Talula and motioned for her to come to him.

She glanced at Mae. "I will come back."

She went to her parents, taking the pond apples with her to make sure the kids didn't eat them.

Jacob put his hand on her shoulder. "You are fluent in the languages."

"Wait," said Ma.

Jacob held up his other hand and shook his head. "Even more so than me. Talula, I need you to—"

"Let us go. I am ready," she said. "When do we leave?"

Tears formed in her mother's eyes, but she didn't say anything further. She strode off after Mae and Tip.

"Ma. . ." Talula watched her walk away. "She will not say goodbye?"

Her pa patted her shoulder. "This is not something that is asked of females. She is worried for you."

"Should I be afraid?"

"No," Jacob responded. "I won't let anything happen to you."

The next morning, Talula and Jacob left without saying goodbye to anyone. Talula was unaware of what awaited her. But she would do whatever her father and her people needed. She held her father's hand. As long as she had him by her side, she could do anything.

Chapter Five

A man led two mares over to Talula and Jacob and rubbed the bay coat of the smaller one. Talula couldn't believe she was going to ride with her father. She had never ridden with him, nor had she had enough riding lessons for her liking.

She hesitated. "This horse does not know me."

Jacob patted the mare's neck. "She will get to know you along the way."

Talula walked along the side of the horse and stepped toward it with her hands out. "I am your friend," she told it. She gently rubbed its neck and shoulder. "We are going for a ride."

For a moment, she thought it nodded.

Jacob helped her up into the saddle, and Talula held the reins. "Do not throw me off."

"She is gentle," said the horseman. "A fine companion for your journey."

Jacob patted Talula's leg, then mounted his horse, and they were off. Talula wondered if Jacob's horse knew where to go as he led the way through the forest.

They traveled north peacefully. There were four other riders who followed, but they never rode with them for long. Once, after leaving, the riders rejoined them with news.

One of them watched Talula as he whispered to Jacob. The only thing she heard was someone was near.

A day later, a group of armed men on horseback came upon Talula and Jacob. The other riders had gone ahead, so Talula and Jacob were alone.

These new men were too far away to see clearly, but they definitely had weapons. A team of horses pulled a wagon behind them. Talula's stomach knotted at the sight of the people crowded inside it.

The man who appeared to be their leader sneered at her and Jacob. "Well, what do we have here?"

"Don't speak," Jacob told Talula.

"I heard him," another armed man said. "That's English, but you're dressed like Ingines."

Talula had never heard the word pronounced that way before. She wanted to ask if he was trying to say Indians, but her father shot her a look.

"What plantation are you from?" the first man asked.

"We are not from a plantation," Jacob replied.

The man rode closer on his horse, looking him over. "It's one of the uppity ones for sure."

The other man leaned in his saddle. "Hey, little girl. What plantation are you from?"

Talula began to speak, but Jacob held his hand out to the side, silencing her. Her mouth hung open. She glanced at the armed man. Now that he was closer, she could see that his face was not white like she thought it would be.

Jacob let go of his reins as the men spread out and cut off the road in both directions.

"Hey, what are you doing? Get down," said the man. "Are there more of you? Are you scouts?"

"No, sir," said Jacob. He dismounted his horse.

"Why are you traveling with an Indian girl?" asked another.

"She is my daughter," said Jacob.

"Get over here. Hurry up. Moving as slow as molasses," the first man said. "Supposedly, free and runaway slaves are given sanctuary here by the Spanish as long as they convert to Catholicism and aid in defending Florida."

Jacob lifted his chin. "We are interpreters."

"For who?" the armed man asked.

"The Seminoles and Creeks. So they can negotiate with Americans."

The closest man looked at Talula. "Is that right, girl?"

She slowly nodded but couldn't take her eyes off the wagon with the cage. The people inside it watched the scene with weary eyes.

The leader put his hand on his hip. "Where did you live before this?"

"I have always lived here," Pa replied.

"He is lying!" A man kicked his horse and rode up to Jacob with a knife drawn and cut his tunic off. He scowled. "No markings on this one."

"Don't worry, we'll take care of that." A man with hateful eyes and a crown of blond hair glowered at Pa.

Jacob turned to Talula. He looked into her eyes.

Run! He yelled. Not aloud, but Talula could hear it in her spirit.

"Yah!" Talula exclaimed. She clung to her horse as it galloped away.

The last thing she saw was her father tussling with one of the men. The one that had a knife, and then she heard shots.

She slowed her horse and looked back. The shots had come from the forest, and she spotted the men who had been riding with her and Jacob earlier hiding in the trees with their guns drawn.

Talula pushed aside her fear and stopped her horse and waited, hoping her father was behind her. But she could hear the men whooping. Their horses' hoofbeats were gaining on her. She clucked to her horse and set off again, but suddenly one of the armed men came from her right. He galloped up beside her and reached for her, sending her off balance. She tumbled off her mare and down the sloping road. There Talula lay, unconscious under the brush.

Talula awoke in the darkness to bobbing lanterns and yells.

The gruff voice of the hunters' leader startled her. "Where is she?"

"She couldn't have gotten far," his comrade replied.

She held her breath, hoping they wouldn't find her.

"Those Ingines eyes pierce the dark. She can see all right."

"Find her before she comes back with more of them."

"He said she's his daughter."

"You saw her. She's dressed like those Seminoles. That wasn't his daughter. He's a slave trying to hide."

Talula's head ached, but she crawled away and climbed the nearest tree and watched the men as they rode beneath her. They stopped not far off, looking around, and then split up.

She waited all night in the tree. At dawn, she made sure all was quiet, then took off like a shot from a musket. She didn't look back, and she didn't stop until there wasn't enough air in her lungs to take another breath.

Thick brush and tangled branches scraped against her and pulled at her hair as she pushed forward. Talula breathed a sigh of relief when she reached an area of open land. Then she noticed the animal carcasses that lay nearby. She recognized the field she'd stopped in, though the many cattle that had been there before were gone.

Talula lifted her skirt and ran. She was almost home. She reached the path that led to her village, but at its entrance she fell to her knees and screamed out to the Breathmaker. The village had been burned down. Smoke still hung in the air and there was a charred scent Talula was not accustomed to. And nothing remained of their settlement's crops.

A soft moan came from her, and she placed her dirt-stained hands over her mouth, trying to make it stop as she forced herself to continue on. After a few struggling steps, she turned around to take one last look at what used to be her home. The scene made her wearier than she'd been while traveling through the dense forest. But she knew if she didn't keep going, she'd never see her family again.

Talula went to the oak tree she'd hidden her bow and arrows in. She climbed its branches. They were still there.

She prayed to the Breathmaker to give her strength before she set out again.

The men must have taken her father, or he would have found her. She refused to believe that anything worse than that had happened to him. She had wanted to help him—to fight for him like the Seminole warriors. If only she'd had an arrow or a spear.

As she walked, she heard voices. Low and faint. Singing. She couldn't tell what direction the song came from. She closed her eyes and listened. Something about how the river flows and learning along the bank. She went to the river and waited where she'd had her lesson.

Talula groggily opened her eyes to the road passing below her as she floated by. She shook her head, forcing herself fully awake. Her body bounced in time with the clopping of hooves, and a warm hide was beneath her. She startled, realizing she was slung over the back of a horse.

"Whoa," said the rider.

Talula struggled to sit straight behind him.

"You woke?" he asked, giving her a hand.

"Pa!" she exclaimed.

"No, not Pa." He glanced over his shoulder. It was the young man with an African accent. "It is I, Amos. I cannot believe someone so small survived."

"What happened?" Talula asked, now fully alert.

"We got away, but we had to leave some of the others behind," he said sadly. "You heard the song. You knew where to go."

"Who sang it?"

"Your father started it. The others joined in."

Talula's heart ached. "Where have those hunters taken Pa? I have to find him."

Amos pressed his lips together. "Hold still, little one. It is not so easy."

Dragonflies lay their eggs in water, and when the larvae hatch, they live underwater for up to two years. Depending on the altitude and latitude, some species may stay in the larval state for up to six years. They'll molt up to seventeen times as they grow and get ready to head to the surface to transform into the dragonflies we see in the air.

Chapter Six

Talula's muscles tightened as she stared at the campfire. She wanted to rescue Jacob immediately. As she focused on the flickering flames, she thought of how her life used to be before she saw that smoke pluming over the trees. She missed her family, the villagers—they were her family too. She began to remember all the things she'd learned from the boys she'd tracked many mornings. Her eyes widened as her path suddenly became clear to her. This was why she was so different from the other girls—her destiny.

If it were a boy, determined to find his father and setting out on his own, it would be okay. Like a rite of passage. She was not yet a woman, but she was strong. There was no doubt in her mind that she could do it.

"What are you thinking, little one?" asked Amos from his seat across the fire. "I can tell you are not like the others. It is because part of you is us and part of you is Seminole. It is well." He attempted to smile, but it didn't reach his eyes.

Talula only stared at him and the others around the fire. Tears stung her eyes. Amos held his head in his hands. He had been the only one that had spoken. Despite his injuries, he had managed to come up with a plan to rescue Jacob. It was good, but there was nothing about it that would help Talula immediately.

The campfire burned down with only a few embers fighting to stay lit. Everyone went to turn in for the night. Talula was left alone in the darkness to think.

It was time for her to go. She knew what she must do. She rose to leave and found Amos blocking her path.

"No, Talula."

Talula's heart dropped like a stone to the bottom of a deep river. Amos would never let her go. She knew he was only trying to protect her. More tears welled in her eyes.

"I must—"

"No," said Amos

"The villages need my father. He unites them and us with the Seminoles. I think I know how to help my father."

Amos sent the other men off and took Talula to the nearest Black Seminole village. As they entered it, he told her, "Do not speak until I have explained everything."

Talula nodded.

Amos instructed that she wait outside one of the cabins as he went in to speak to the village leaders.

A short while later, he brought several others outside with him.

A broad-shouldered man looked her over from the cabin steps. "A child who knows their language better than we? And she understands American writings. Is it true?"

"Yes," said Amos, who stepped down around him.

"Fetch her," said another Black Seminole who stood with the leader.

Talula approached them.

The leader peered at her closely. "Is this true?"

She nodded. "Yes."

A man who claimed to be the village's translator glared at her. "You lie."

She'd never met him before, but right off, she didn't like him or the way he looked down his nose at her.

The Black Seminoles started to talk among themselves as if she wasn't there.

Talula exhaled sharply. She moved her gaze to the leader and spoke in English, Creek, Mikasuki, and Spanish. "They call themselves Patriots," she told them.

Then she knelt and wrote the words in the soil though her spelling was not perfect. "I do not lie."

The translator lowered his voice and spoke to the leader.

After a few seconds, he looked at her. "Your father is Jacob."

"Yes."

Murmurs came from all around them.

Talula lifted her chin. "I am going to save him, and I need your help."

There were a few snickers from the others, but the leader did not laugh.

"I will do it with you or without you," she said. "In saving him, we will save all of our people."

One of the other men from the cabin crossed his arms. "Are you going to listen to this little ant?"

Talula stood tall and spoke from her heart. "Listen to me. I have no fear."

"Have you a plan?" he asked.

She gestured to the leader. "I'll need your help to free them. We will free our people and unite them."

"That is impossible. Our people are scattered," said another man.

The Black Seminole leader stood up and stared at her. He glanced at the gathered men. "Do you know where they are?"

"St. Augustine," said Amos.

"You are certain?"

"Yes."

The leader looked away and rubbed his chin. "The fort."

Talula didn't understand what he meant.

He turned back to her with a serious look. "We will do what you ask. I will be your help."

"Thank you," she said.

"What is your name?" he asked.

"Talula."

"What is that word?"

"It is Seminole, given to me by my grandmother. It means one who leaps water." She stomped her foot. "And I will leap over the enemy."

The leader smirked and studied her. "You're not going. You will be safe here."

"I must go!" Talula exclaimed. "Seminole warriors have agreed to join us. I must interpret."

His brows rose.

"She is a child!" said the other man. "These are lies!"

Talula's mother appeared behind her with the Seminole warriors Amos had sent for.

She stepped to Talula's side, her face proud. "She does not lie."

The village leader stared at her mother, then dipped his head. "Talula, I will listen to you. The rest of us will listen to you. If you take us to where Jacob is, we will bring him home."

"Thank you, ❖ Prince Witten."

❖ A joint force of two hundred Seminole warriors and forty Black Seminole fighters struck the northern plantations along the river.

Just outside of St. Augustine, they heard the first sign of the existence of the Patriot army. Voices, strong and clear, drifted through the night from not far off.

The forces surrounded the Patriot camp, and Prince Witten held up his hand for them to wait.

Talula recognized the hat of one of the men as he went into a tent. She tore away from her group and knelt behind the tent to listen.

Amos crouched low in the brush behind her. He put his hands out, telling her to wait there.

A deep voice came from inside the tent. "These Black Seminole settlements could put an end to the slave system. And the relationship between these Red and Black Seminoles—they're devoted to each other in some way."

"Yes, but that one out back, he's not like the others," another male voice replied. "He's educated or something. It's against the law to educate slaves. Someone has taught him."

"That slave hasn't been to any school—"

The sound of hundreds of footsteps pounded through the air, and the soldiers charged outside.

People ran in every direction, fleeing the camp.

"They're running free! Who unchained them? C'mere," a soldier shouted as he grabbed at a man who broke free of his grasp.

Black Seminoles and Seminole warriors fought for their lives as the slave women and children ran for the swamp. The fight went on for hours and the Patriots' tents were set afire.

Though Talula was supposed to stay away from the fighting—she'd been promised they would free her father—she ran around the edge of the attack zone, trying to find him.

Everywhere she looked, there was fire, yelling, and smoke. Men fought all around her, and she remembered her mother's words not to watch war— "What the eye sees and gives to the mind damages the soul."

She kept her eyes low and was glad she did. She came upon a bow and a quiver of arrows. Thinking it a sign, she picked them up and slung the quiver over her shoulder. Near the wagons, a few Patriots guarded a group of slaves who were still tied up. At the sight of the fight, some of the Patriots deserted their posts and ran into the forest.

Jacob saw Talula at the same time as the man guarding him. He looked around for a weapon.

"Let him go." Talula pointed the bow to the sky and stared at her target.

"Do not underestimate her," came Jacob's voice. "She is my child."

The guard smirked at her and drew his sword.

Talula moved swiftly. She brought the bow down, drawing the arrow at the same time, then aimed it and let go. The arrow whizzed through the air and pierced the guard's leg.

"Run, Talula!" Jacob shouted.

dulichia

Talula turned to run but stopped, refusing to leave her father behind again. She bit her lip and drew another arrow. She ran toward Jacob, passing the guard who had fallen to the ground, clutching his leg.

Jacob rose with the men he was tied to. "Do what I told you!" he shouted at them.

They moved together as one person as Jacob pulled back his shoulder and they charged into the Patriots behind Talula. In all the chaos, she hadn't heard them approaching.

The soldiers yelled as Jacob and the enslaved men hit them square, falling atop them.

A soldier came running up behind them with a musket.

"Talula!" Jacob yelled.

Talula aimed her arrow, but at the sound of her name, she hesitated.

The patriot fired the musket but missed, hitting a tree behind Talula.

Talula gasped. She readied her arrow again as the man revealed a knife.

Just as he began to charge toward her, a group of Seminole warriors ran over and grabbed him. One of them untied Jacob and the other slaves.

Talula lowered the bow and dropped it on the ground. She ran to her father and threw her arms around him. "Are you okay?"

"I'm fine." Jacob grunted. "You have to go."

"I can't leave you."

As she spoke, another patriot came out of nowhere. In seconds, Jacob leapt onto the soldier and wrestled him to the ground. Jacob took his blade from him and held it to his neck.

"The time for this is over," Jacob said. "Go back to your plantation and do not come back."

Jacob got off of him. The man nodded as he backed away.

Jacob grabbed Talula around the waist, then lifted her into the air and took her to safety as the remaining Patriots retreated. He didn't stop running until he came upon Seminole Indians. He held Talula to him and didn't cry but let out a wail into her hair that sent shivers up her spine. Then, he fell silent and set her down.

"Thank you," he told the Seminoles. "Thank you," he said as he turned to Amos and the Black Seminoles with him.

The group of fighters from the village gathered around him.

He looked exhausted, but still he shouted, "We're never going back to Georgia!"

Everybody cheered, throwing their hands holding muskets and spears in the air.

Jacob turned his head sharply to look at Talula, then spoke with an unaccustomed edge to his voice. "This is our home. We will build again."

Talula smiled through her tears as Jacob embraced her. They walked ahead along the road from St. Augustine with their group, heading home. Talula's mother followed, helping with the women and children who'd run to the swamp.

"Our fight is over for now," Jacob told Talula as they walked.

"Do you think they will come back?" Talula replied.

Jacob's gaze fell to the left. He pointed at the ocean through the trees.

Massive sails were visible through the foliage.

Talula gasped. "Ships! Pa, what is on those ships?"

Jacob didn't respond. He stopped, and so did everyone behind him.

He signaled, and Amos ran up to them. He motioned his head toward the ocean. "Send the scouts."

Amos nodded and set off.

After that, Jacob walked in silence beside Talula for a long while.

She could see there was much on his mind. "Pa, do you hear the drums again?"

He smiled. "I heard them as soon as I saw you."

Talula grinned.

After a few minutes of silence, she cleared her throat. "Pa, why do they hate us?"

He rubbed his chin and thought for a moment. A dragonfly flitted above their heads, and he stared at it. "Some things are harder to explain to a child than the way the river flows.

"Or the flight of a dragonfly."

Chapter Seven

The light from the projector flickered as the film ended.

Mia wriggled on her seat. "Wow."

"Right?" her father replied.

"That was epic! Is all of that true?"

Mr. Emathla's voice came from behind them. "We had to use a little creative license. But for the most part, yes."

Paisley stood. "Yeah, it's not like someone wrote down everything that happened back then."

Mr. Emathla came out from behind the wall. "True. But thank goodness some events were documented. We've been able to retrieve factual evidence."

While the adults talked about the events of the film, Mia thought about Talula and her determination to keep her people alive. She tried to imagine what it would be like to live in Florida back then. No buildings, cities, or streetlights. The state would've been mostly jungle and swamp.

There was a crack of thunder, and the lights flickered.

"That was close, wasn't it?" Mia asked Paisley.

She hugged herself with wide eyes. "I think it shook the room."

"Don't worry girls, the storm will blow over soon," said Mia's mother.

"Let's head into the next area," said Mr. Emathla. "There's more to see."

They all got up from their seats and followed him out of the theater.

Suddenly, it sounded like a dump truck plowed through the building. Mia and Paisley screamed and ducked as the roof tore open and oak tree branches plunged inside.

"That's the big oak beside the building. Is everyone all right? Here," Mr. Emathla said with his hand outstretched. "Walk along the walls."

They all scurried to the side of the hallway, and Mia pulled out her phone and turned it on, checking the screen. "I think it's a tornado. Our phones were on silent. There's a severe weather alert."

"Look at how dark the sky is," Paisley said, pointing. Thunder boomed again, and all the lights went out in the facility. Debris flew at the windows.

"Follow me," Mr. Emathla yelled. He switched on the light from his keychain.

Suddenly, the thundering stopped. So did the wind and rain. Silence fell over them.

"I think we need to get out of here," said Mia.

"We can't. It's too dangerous," Paisley whined and clasped Mia's hand.

"What do you think is happening, a tropical storm?" asked her mother.

"No. I'm pretty sure there's a tornado nearing the museum," her father replied, looking at his phone.

"No!" Mia cried out.

"Yes," Mr. Emathla agreed. He shielded his eyes from the dust and debris blowing in through the roof. "Listen, we are not safe where we are. We have to get to the other side of the building."

"We can't possibly run away from a tornado. It's faster than any of us," said Mia.

"Yeah, but we can find a better place to protect ourselves." He waved his arm. "This way! We have to crawl under the debris to get to the lobby."

Just as they began to crawl, the sound of a train tore through the air, followed by a loud cracking noise.

"Mia, crawl!"

It was as if the tornado had ripped the words out of her parents' mouths.

"Paisley!" Mia yelled, looking for her friend.

Paisley wasn't answering. The howling and the whistle of the tornado grew louder. Mia covered her ears.

The building shook and debris shot through the air. Mia stared at her mom next to her. Her eyes were wide with fear.

Mia tried to crawl but collapsed under an explosion of boards and rubble. She opened her eyes but couldn't see anyone. "Daddy," she cried.

But he didn't respond, nor did her mother. She found Paisley's limp arm beside her under the wreckage.

She heard her mother's weak moan and pushed at the twisted metal and busted drywall with all of her might.

I have to help them, she thought. *Like Talula.* But Mia never thought of herself as brave. She wasn't a survivor or a warrior. She didn't stick up for herself at school, and she was never a leader.

"Keep going, Mia," she told herself. She pushed again, and the debris shifted. She fought to crawl out of the rubble and found herself alone outside.

The parking lot was a mass of destruction, just like the museum. Twisted, broken metal lay scattered on the pavement.

"Where is our car?"

She ran to the road, jumping over tree limbs brought down by the tornado, and didn't stop running until she flagged down a truck.

Fire trucks and ambulances pulled up to the museum with their sirens blaring and lights flashing. Mia showed them where she had crawled out, where her family and Paisley were still trapped inside. The rescuers bent over and shined their lights all over the area, revealing the damage and destroyed artifacts.

A beam caught on her mother's limping form.

"There!" said Mia.

Mr. Emathla was with her, helping her and Paisley get outside. Paisley was conscious and crying.

Both adults had injuries to their heads.

The paramedics put her mother and Paisley onto stretchers and loaded them into the ambulances.

Mr. Emathla stood outside with a few police officers and firemen, explaining what happened. They wanted to make sure no one was missing.

"Where is my dad?" Mia got off the ambulance and tried to step outside, but Mr. Emathla caught her by the arm. "Mia, no. The building isn't safe to enter again. Wait and let the firemen do what they're trained to do."

Mia watched the firemen. They shined their lights under the wreckage, searched inside the standing part of the building but didn't come out with her father.

"There's no one in there that we can see," the fire chief stated. "We have to remove the debris."

"Yes, there is someone in there!" Mia yelled. She jumped down from the ambulance and ran to the hole she'd come out of.

"Mia, no! Stop!" Mr. Emathla followed her, but he couldn't catch her.

Mia ignored him and crawled inside.

The air was thin, making it hard to breathe. She coughed and kept crawling. It was so dark she couldn't see, but she didn't care. Her heart beat so hard she was afraid it would burst.

Someone grabbed her arm.

"Dad?" she coughed and wheezed, squinting in the darkness. She felt the hand clutching her. It was wide and rough.

"He's here!" she tried to yell, but her voice was scarcely more than a whisper.

The next thing Mia knew, she was being pulled out.

"I'm here!" a voice shouted. She was sure it was her father's.

His hand slid from her arm, but someone shined a light into the hole and her dad's face lit up in front of her. He crawled after her.

"Dad!"

"Mia."

"I thought. . ."

"Yes."

"I thought—I thought—" She broke into sobs.

"I'm right here," he said as the paramedics carefully pulled her. "I'm not going anywhere."

Suddenly, she was outside. Someone cradled her head while a paramedic wrapped her in a blanket. She tried to open her eyes, but it was too bright.

"Can you hear me?" a paramedic asked.

"My name is Anthony. Can you tell me your name?"

Mia blinked a few times to clear her vision. She could just make out a man leaning over her.

"Mia." Her voice was hoarse. She looked to the right, seeing her father on a stretcher. Their eyes met, and he spoke to her without saying a word.

Mia grinned and closed her eyes. She'd saved her family. Just like Talula.

As she was lifted into the ambulance, she thought of the warrior girl.

Talula. One who leaps water. The name of a legendary Black Seminole warrior. I'm like her. Maybe one day my ancestors will tell stories passed down through generations of a brave African American warrior named Mia. Talula and Mia.

Mia rubbed her fingers over her stomach. When no one was looking, she'd picked up Talula's painting, held it to her chest and zipped it inside her jacket before she'd continued crawling. "Our history must live on."

Definitions

Micco = chief

Talwa = tribal town

Chickee = an open-sided structure, usually thatched with palms and serving as a dwelling

Seminole = the Spanish word for "runaways" or "wild ones". *Cimarrónes*
(https://www.semtribe.com/stof/history/introduction)

Black Seminole = also called Seminole Maroons or Seminole Freedmen, a group of free Blacks and runaway slaves (maroons) that joined forces with the Seminole Indians in Florida from approximately 1700 through the 1850s. The Black Seminoles were celebrated for their bravery and tenacity during the three Seminole Wars.
(https://www.britannica.com/topic/Black-Seminoles)

More to Know

Chapter Two

❖Juan Caballo aka JOHN HORSE
Born a slave of African American, Indian, and Spanish descent in 1812 in Florida, John Horse (Juan Caballo, Juan Cavallo, and often Gopher John) rose to become one of the most successful Black freedom fighters in American history.

In his lifetime, he fought as a sub-chief during the Second Seminole War, served as a decorated officer in the Mexican military, and met two presidents. He defended free Black settlements on three frontiers and spent the majority of his life on a quest to secure a free homeland for his people in Mexico.
(https://www.seminolenationmuseum.org/history/seminole-nation/john-horse/)

Chapter Three

❖William Powell aka OSCEOLA

Powell adopted the name Osceola, which means "Black drink crier", at a tribal ceremony around 1820. Osceola was named Billy Powell at birth in 1804 in the Creek village of Talisi, now known as Tallassee, Alabama, in current Elmore County. "The people in the town of Tallassee were mixed-blood Native American/English/Irish/Scottish, and some were Black. Billy was all of these."

After the Red Stick Creek were defeated by United States forces, Osceola's mother, Polly, took him and moved with other Creek refugees from Alabama to Florida, where they joined the Seminole.

In adulthood, as part of the Seminole, Powell was given his name Osceola. This is an anglicized form of the Creek Asi-yahola, the combination of asi, the ceremonial black drink made from the yaupon holly, and yahola, meaning "shout" or "shouter." (https://nativeheritageproject.com/2014/05/10/seminole-chief-osceola-billy-powell/)

Chapter Six

❖Prince Witten

Prince Witten, apparently born about 1756 in South Carolina, had escaped from Georgia to Spanish St. Augustine with his family around 1786, after several previously failed attempts. The skilled carpenter registered in 1798 with Florida Governor Vincent Manuel de Zéspedes as required, and soon hired himself out as a carpenter in the area. By 1801 Witten had become a captain of the Florida Black militia when his son-in-law Jorge Jacobo assumed command of the unit.

In late July, a Black man traveling throughout Florida warned both Seminole and Black Seminole villages that an attack was underway, and that Whites planned to take their land and subdue them. On July 25, two hundred Indian warriors and forty Blacks from the Alachua region attacked the plantations along the St. Johns River, causing panic and desertion among the Georgia militia. Slaves deserted plantations throughout the region as well as in Georgia and South Carolina to join the Indian and Black warriors.

(Porter, Kenneth W, 'The Black Seminoles: History of a Freedom Seeking People,' University Press of Florida, 1996.)

Thereafter, Witten distinguished himself, winning accolades from his Spanish rulers and disdain and contempt from his American enemies. Witten commanded the local Black militia when they won the most important engagement of the Patriot War in September 1812, and by doing so, he achieved the distinction of becoming a Black officer.

In order to prevent the influx of Black troops and supplies into St. Augustine, the United States instituted a blockade on the upper peninsula of East Florida. Their aim was to destroy St. Augustine by first reducing the strength of the garrison by cutting off the supply line, followed by an assault on the garrison, thus rendering the city defeated. Those plans were thwarted on September 12 by the group of Blacks and Indians led by Prince Witten.

(https://www.nps.gov/articles/sanctuary-in-the-spanish-empire.htm)

Chapter Three

❖In the early 1800s, Great Britain was fighting a war against France. The United States did not take part in this war, but Britain tried to keep U.S. ships from stopping at French ports. The British also took sailors away from U.S. ships and forced them to join the British Navy. These actions angered many people in the United States.

People who lived in newly settled areas of the United States were also angry with Britain. They accused the British of getting Native Americans to attack settlers.
(https://kids.britannica.com/kids/article/War-of-1812/353909)

Chapter Six

❖Following the War of 1812 between the United States and Britain, American slave owners came to Florida in search of runaway African slaves and Indians. These Indians, known as the Seminole, and the runaway slaves had been trading weapons with the British throughout the early 1800s and supported Britain during the War of 1812. From 1817-1818, the United States Army invaded Spanish Florida and fought against the Seminole and their African American allies. Collectively,

these battles came to be known as the First
Seminole War.
(http://www.pbchistoryonline.org/middle-school-lessons/014-
SeminoleWars/014-Seminole-Wars1.htm)

Acknowledgments and Sources

Thank you to the wonderful 4th and 5th grade 2021 students of Azalea Elementary School in St. Petersburg, Florida for creating the character, Paisley.

I couldn't have written this book without my beta readers who believed so much in this project, the Ah-Tah-Thi-Ki Museum, and the following resources:

Loren, William Kate, 'Black Indians: A Hidden Heritage,' The Atheneum Books for Young Readers, 2012.

Porter, Kenneth W, 'The Black Seminoles: History of a Freedom-Seeking People,' University Press of Florida, 1996.

Seminolenationmuseum.org
Nativeheritageproject.com
www.treehugger.com/things-you-never-knew-about-dragonflies

A portion of all sales of this book will be donated to the National Black Cultural Information Trust and the Ah-Tah-Thi-Ki Museum.

Please Leave A Review

Your review means the world to me. I greatly appreciate any kind words. Even one or two sentences go a long way. The number of reviews a book receives greatly improves how well it does on Amazon or other online bookstores. Even a short review would be wonderful. Thank you in advance.

Use the QR code below to download your FREE teacher guide!

Author Note

This story is a work of fiction, but some of the characters mentioned actually existed and the setting is very much as it would have been during the 1800s.

Writing this book was an adventure. I researched the history of Black Seminoles for two years before I sat down to write. Interest in my own Indigenous history was a catalyst. The story is from my imagination except where noted with further explanation. Talula may not have been a real person, but the experiences of runaway slaves, freedmen, and Black Seminoles are accurate. There were many historical events that I had to leave out as this is a book for children, but I hope I did my African and Creek ancestors justice.

About The Author

L. B. Anne is best known for her Sheena Meyer book series about a girl with a special gift, and a destiny that can save the world. L. B. Anne lives on the Gulf Coast of Florida with her husband and is a full-time author, speaker, and mental health advocate. When she's not inventing new obstacles for her diverse characters to overcome, you can find her reading, playing bass guitar, running on the beach, or downing a mocha iced coffee at a local cafe while dreaming of being your favorite author. Visit L. B. at www.lbanne.com

Facebook: facebook.com/authorlbanne
Instagram: Instagram.com/authorlbanne
Twitter: twitter.com/authorlbanne
Pinterest: pinterest.com/AuthorLBAnne